I celebrated World Book Day 2018
with this brilliant gift from my local
Bookseller and Puffin Books.

CELEBRATE STORIES. LOVE READING.

This book has been specially written and published to celebrate **World Book Day**. We are a charity who offers every child and young person the opportunity to read and love books by offering you the chance to have a book of your own. To find out more, as well as oodles of fun activities and reading recommendations to continue your reading journey, visit **worldbookday.com**

World Book Day in the UK and Ireland is made possible by generous sponsorship from National Book Tokens, participating publishers, booksellers, authors and illustrators. The £1 book tokens are a gift from your local Bookseller.

World Book Day works in partnership with a number of charities, all of whom are working to encourage a love of reading for pleasure.

The National Literacy Trust is an independent charity that encourages children to enjoy reading. Just 10 minutes of reading every day can make a big difference to how well you do at school and to how successful you could be in life. **literacytrust.org.uk**

The Reading Agency inspires people of all ages and backgrounds to read for pleasure and empowerment. They run the Summer Reading Challenge in partnership with libraries, as well as supporting reading groups in schools and libraries all year round. Find out more and join your local library. **summerreadingchallenge.org.uk**

World Book Day also facilitates fundraising for:

Book Aid International, an international book donation and library development charity. Every year, they provide one million books to libraries and schools in communities where children would otherwise have little or no opportunity to read. **bookaid.org.uk**

Read for Good, who motivate children in schools to read for fun through its sponsored read, which thousands of schools run on World Book Day and throughout the year. The money raised provides new books and resident storytellers in all of the UK's children's hospitals. **readforgood.org**

*€1.50 in Ireland

CLARE BALDING

Illustrated by TONY ROSS

The Girl Who Thought She Was A Dog

PUFFIN

PUFFIN BOOKS

UK | USA | Canada | Ireland | Australia
India | New Zealand | South Africa

Puffin Books is part of the Penguin Random House group of companies
whose addresses can be found at global.penguinrandomhouse.com.

www.penguin.co.uk   www.puffin.co.uk   www.ladybird.co.uk

First published 2018

001

Text copyright © Clare Balding, 2018
Illustrations copyright © Tony Ross, 2018
Extract from *Emmeline and the Plucky Pup* copyright © Megan Rix, 2018

The moral right of the author and illustrator has been asserted

Set in Baskerville MT Std
Printed in Great Britain by Clays Ltd, St Ives plc

A CIP catalogue record for this book is available from the British Library

ISBN: 978-0-241-32373-1

All correspondence to:
Puffin Books
Penguin Random House Children's
80 Strand, London WC2R 0RL

For Archie and all the other dogs
who have brought joy into my life

Chapter One

A New Arrival

They say that all dogs are born with different personalities. Terriers love to dig and will often go missing for hours, disappearing down a tunnel after the faintest glimpse of a rabbit's tail. Greyhounds like to run in short, sharp bursts – and then happily sleep on the sofa for the rest of the day. Dalmatians were bred as carriage dogs and they love to trot alongside a

1

horse or a jogger. With their funny faces and daft behaviour, boxers give the impression of being the jokers of the pack. But they're serious about one thing: boxers are born to protect.

So when Twiglet the boxer's owner, Rosie, brought home an unfamiliar basket one day, he was immediately on his guard. Something inside was making a *tremendous* noise.

Twiglet walked warily around the small basket, sniffing cautiously. Finally, he peered inside and there it was! A tiny human puppy, its face as wrinkled as a prune, screeching like a cat on the attack. He drew back his head in shock.

'It's all right, Twiglet,' said Rosie, bending down to stroke his head. 'She's only a baby. She won't bite.'

Twiglet wasn't so sure. He nervously took a second look. As he did, the baby stopped crying, reached out a tiny hand and grabbed his ear.

Twiglet yelped.

'Oh, sweetheart, I'm sorry!' said Rosie, gently prying the baby's fingers apart to release Twiglet's ear. 'She didn't mean to hurt you.'

Hmm, thought Twiglet. *She doesn't know her own strength.*

Rosie carried the basket into the sitting room, and sank down into the sofa. Twiglet jumped up beside her and nestled into her chest, just as he had done every night for the past two years. He thought she looked exhausted.

'We're in this for the long haul, Twiglet,' Rosie sighed, closing her eyes. 'It's up to you and me to teach this little lady about life.'

Twiglet cocked his ear. Now *that* was

something he could do. Lead the baby in the right direction. Show her how to smell good and bad people, how to play fetch, how to chase a squirrel and how to swallow a whole bowl of food without chewing. Oh, yes, he would be an *excellent* teacher.

'What do you think of the name Fennel?'

Twiglet put his head on one side as he looked up at Rosie. He knew Doris the dachshund, Betty the cockerpoo and Jess the Great Dane. He'd met a William and a Colin and a Dougal but he'd never met a Fennel.

'For the baby, I mean. I don't want her to have the same name as all the other girls. She needs to stand out. She's special!'

Rosie smiled lovingly at the baby, peacefully asleep in her basket. Twiglet thought it was good to see Rosie happy again – even if she did look tired. The baby gurgled contentedly in her sleep and Twiglet wagged his tail.

'Good,' said Rosie. 'Then Fennel it is.'

Later that night, baby Fennel started to cry again. Before she could wake Rosie, Twiglet padded over to Fennel's basket. The baby reached up and, this time, Twiglet didn't shy away, letting her touch his ear and the soft skin round his mouth. Her cries settled down to soft whimpers, and eventually she fell back to sleep.

*

With his keen boxer instincts, Twiglet quickly became Fennel's guardian. The first time Rosie took Fennel for a walk round the park he even growled at Betty the cockerpoo because she bounded up too fast. He told the other dogs to be gentle with her and stuck to Fennel's side the whole morning, only leaving her to quickly do his business under a bush.

When they got back to the house, he sniffed Fennel all over to check she was in tip-top condition. She gurgled happily, snuffling at his fur. Rosie looked on fondly and Twiglet could tell she was glad that the two of them were such fast friends.

Twiglet didn't like it when strange humans came too close to Fennel's basket, and liked it even less when they picked her up and made stupid cooing noises in her face.

They don't even let her sniff them first, and

that's just rude, he thought to himself.

'Twiglet, don't growl!' said Rosie. 'You know Grandma. She's not going to do Fennel any harm.'

Twiglet did know Grandma so he stopped growling, but he kept his eyes on her as she sat Fennel on her lap. He lay down at Grandma's feet and pretended to go to sleep. He didn't really, of course; he just closed his eyes and let his ears move left and right, listening out for any dangerous noises.

'He's very protective,' said Rosie. 'Even when we go for a walk, he won't leave Fennel's side. Lord knows what he'll be like when I start taking her to baby groups. He'll probably try to come too!'

'What about when you go back to work, dear? What's your plan then?' asked Grandma.

'Well, you know I can't afford child care or a nanny . . .' Twiglet heard a pleading note enter Rosie's voice. 'I was hoping you might be able to help me out?'

'And get to spend even more time with Twiglet too?' Grandma gave a delighted laugh and clapped her hands together. 'I'd love to. And I'm sure your brother would be happy to offer his services as well.'

Twiglet knew that Fennel's Uncle James and his partner, Matt, were great fun (they always brought him a bone whenever they came to visit), so he relaxed a little, knowing that he and Fennel would be in good hands.

Chapter Two

First Words

'My granddaughter is a delight!' Grandma beamed. 'Babysitting her is just like looking after a dog. I even found her trying to eat one of Twiglet's biscuits this morning, if you can believe that!'

Rosie frowned. Fennel looked up at her and lazily let her tongue hang out from the corner of her mouth, just like Twiglet did.

'I suppose it's not surprising when she spends so much time with him . . .' Rosie said. 'But I hope you gave her a proper biscuit instead.'

It had been a year since she'd brought Fennel home and her little girl and Twiglet had become the best of friends.

'Oh, I don't think there's anything wrong with being a bit dog,' Grandma said. 'I'd rather be with dogs than humans most of the time!'

Rosie picked up Fennel, who sniffed her behind the ear and then carefully licked her cheek.

'Don't worry, darling,' Grandma chuckled. 'It's just a phase. She'll grow out of it!'

But Fennel didn't grow out of it. As the year went on, Rosie began to observe that Fennel would much rather chase a ball in the garden than listen to a story and, if they were to avoid a tantrum of epic proportions, all her meals had to be served in a metal bowl rather than on a plate. Twiglet seemed to know exactly what Fennel meant if she gave a little bark or a whine but, despite Rosie's best efforts, Fennel had yet to say her first words.

'Mama,' said Rosie, pointing to herself. 'Mama.'

Fennel barked.

'Oh well,' Grandma said, as Rosie's shoulders slumped. 'It'll happen when she's ready!'

One Sunday morning, when two-year-old Fennel was slurping up cereal from her bowl, she suddenly looked up. She pointed at her best friend and said, clear as anything:

'Twiglet!'

Rosie beamed at her. 'Well done, darling! That's Twiglet. And what about me?'

'Twiglet!' Fennel said again.

Rosie laughed and texted her brother:

Fennel just said her first word!

Wow! What did she say? replied Uncle James.

Rosie sent back the answer with a crying-laughing emoji. Her phone pinged straight away with a row of little dogs.

Uncle James and Uncle Matt came over later that day to play with Fennel and took her into the garden to throw her favourite ball.

'Fennel!' Uncle James shouted, when she was over on the other side of the lawn. She bounded towards him on all fours, Twiglet right by her side. Uncle James smiled. 'Look, Matt – she really does act just like a dog!'

Fennel sat on her haunches and looked up at him. Twiglet did the same. Uncle James ruffled Fennel's hair, and then stroked Twiglet's head.

Uncle Matt looked bemused. 'You're right, she does. That's ... err ... different.'

Fennel went over to Uncle Matt's side and he lifted her on to his lap. She curled into his chest and licked his hand. Then she grinned at Twiglet and gave a gruff bark. Uncle James laughed – but Twiglet's heart leaped as he realized she was trying to speak in *his* language.

'Best friends!' she gurgled, in broken Doggish.

Twiglet wagged his tail excitedly and barked back, 'Forever!'

Fennel soon grew into a gentle and obedient toddler. As long as she was near Twiglet, she was never any trouble at all.

But at bedtime it was a different story.

'I don't know what to do,' Rosie said to Grandma, after yet another sleepless night of tears and tantrums. 'She's got a lovely new bed and a beautiful night light but she just won't go to sleep.'

'Have you tried letting Twiglet sleep in her room?' Grandma suggested.

'Oh, I don't think that's a good idea. She's already so dependent on him.'

Grandma shrugged and gave her a knowing look. 'If you're sure . . .'

But after a few more sleepless nights, Rosie was ready to try anything.

'Come on, then, Twiglet,' she said, opening the door to Fennel's room and letting him bound inside. Sure enough, as soon as she had her best friend cuddled up beside her, Fennel's tears stopped.

*

Fennel was becoming more and more like Twiglet as the months passed. Whenever someone came to the house, Fennel would wag her bottom from side to side as if she had an invisible tail. She would occasionally stand up if she wanted to reach something, but mainly she stuck to crawling around on all fours. It seemed that if that was good enough for Twiglet, it was good enough for her.

As much as her mum loved to see her happy, sometimes Rosie had to draw the line.

'FENNEL, NO! Get your face out of there!'

Fennel lifted her face from Twiglet's water bowl in surprise. She had been trying to scoop the water up with the end of her tongue like Twiglet, but human tongues weren't made like a dog's and it was proving impossible. There was water all over the kitchen floor.

'Darling, you are NOT A DOG!'

Rosie's voice came out more firmly than she intended and immediately she could see the tears forming in Fennel's eyes. Fennel slunk away and curled up with Twiglet in his basket, silently crying into his fur.

Twiglet looked at Rosie and shook his head from side to side.

Rosie glared at him. 'Oh, for goodness' sake. Don't *you* start!'

Chapter Three

Human Training

'We need to talk about Fennel.'

Uncle James and Uncle Matt were standing with their arms folded in the sitting room.

'Whatever do you mean?' Grandma said, looking offended.

Rosie put a gentle hand on her arm. 'Look . . .'

They all turned to look at the dog basket,

where Fennel and Twiglet were sitting in quiet companionship. Fennel stretched and started to lick the back of her hand.

Grandma flushed. 'I don't think it's that bad, do you? We all love dogs here.' Twiglet got up and walked towards her, wagging his tail. She took his head in her hands and kissed him on the soft bit of his forehead.

'Well, I'm worried about her,' Uncle James continued. 'Every other child her age is talking. They're at least able to say 'Mama' or 'Dada'. She can only say 'Twiglet' and bark. She eats her food out of a bowl, without using her hands, let alone cutlery. I'm not sure Fennel understands that she's a human being at all. She thinks she's a dog.'

Grandma sniffed. 'It's probably because Rosie gave her a name that rhymes with kennel!'

Rosie caught her brother's eye. The two of

them started giggling while Uncle Matt struggled to keep a straight face.

'It might sound funny now,' Uncle James said gently, 'but it won't be funny when she goes to school and the other parents see her behaving like a dog. They won't want her round to play with their kids if she's likely to growl at them and cock her leg on the tulips!'

Twiglet was listening to all this with his head on one side. Uncle James had a point. Twiglet knew that he couldn't be Fennel's *only* friend. And if she was going to make new friends, he would have to help her act more like a human.

Twiglet knew that Fennel was learning English just as quickly as she was picking up Doggish. She just needed to practise a bit more. So the next day, after they had both had their tea and he had let her win tug-of-war with a rope, Twiglet took Fennel into the garden and explained that her family were worried she was acting too much like a dog.

'You've got to be more human,' he said, as kindly as he could.

'Why?' Fennel sniffed. 'Fennel and Twiglet. Dogs together.'

'I know – I get it!' Twiglet replied. 'And we'll always be together. But you have to try to make human friends, otherwise you won't fit in.'

Twiglet had seen the way humans often seemed to be scared of being different. They dressed the same, did their hair the same, ate the same food, watched the same TV programmes, went on holiday to the same places, even painted their walls the same shade of cream.

'Want to be a dog,' Fennel insisted, crinkling her brow.

'I know,' said Twiglet, 'but dogs don't rule

the world – humans do! And for your own sake, you need to try a bit harder to be like one.'

They were interrupted by Rosie walking into the garden. 'What are you two up to?'

Fennel and Twiglet exchanged a glance.

'Mama!' said Fennel loudly, reaching up with her arms.

Rosie hugged her tight, closing her eyes with glee. 'Oh, you little star!' she said, swinging her round. 'You clever, clever girl. Isn't she brilliant, Twiglet?'

Twiglet wagged his tail. *Excellent*, he thought. *It's working.*

When they went to the park the next day with Grandma and Uncle James, Fennel put her new resolve to the test.

Most toddlers would point at Twiglet and say, 'Doggy!' Their parents always looked proud and praised them for their mastery of the English language. Fennel couldn't understand what the big deal was. Of course it was a 'doggy', but what breed was it? Fennel's knowledge was far more advanced – she and Grandma often spent entire evenings watching old YouTube videos of Crufts. She pointed at different dogs and said:

'Whippet. Border terrier. Poodle.'

Sometimes she added a bit more detail.

'Ugly pug. Fat Labrador.'

'Fennel, shh!' Grandma blushed and mumbled her apologies to the dogs' horrified owners.

'She's the brightest toddler in town,' Uncle James said proudly. 'That Labrador was definitely on the podgy side . . .'

Chapter Four

Guard Duty

Fennel was growing into a healthy little girl. She had a short bout of kennel cough when she was four (the doctor diagnosed it as whooping cough but Twiglet knew better). She learned to eat politely around others, but back home she was completely herself, imitating Twiglet as he dug in the soil or rolled in grass cuttings.

Every six weeks or so, Fennel needed to have her hair trimmed. She hated it and usually threw a full-scale tantrum, so one weekend Rosie came up with a plan – if Twiglet went to the hairdresser without a fuss, maybe Fennel would too.

The only problem was that Twiglet didn't need to have his hair cut regularly like a cockerpoo or a Tibetan terrier – his hair was short and it moulted.

'We don't normally get boxers coming in,' said the receptionist at Dogs' Delight.

'I know,' said Rosie, keeping her voice down. 'He doesn't need a cut, obviously, but a shampoo and dry would be great and maybe a nail trim as well?'

The receptionist nodded, and led Twiglet off to start the treatment.

'Look, darling!' said Rosie. 'Twiglet is off to

get his hair cut and *he's* not making a fuss, is he?'

She led Fennel next door to the hairdresser. 'You and Twiglet should be ready at exactly the same time. And I'll tell you what – if you're a good girl, we can go to the park afterwards.'

Fennel hesitated in the doorway, but as Twiglet was going through the same experience, she figured she had better be brave as well.

'OK, Mama,' she said, and trotted inside.

Forty minutes later, they were both ready.

'Park, Mama,' Fennel reminded her mum firmly, and it wasn't long before she and Twiglet were rolling on the cricket pitch, trying to replace the smell of shampoo with that of freshly cut grass.

They were happily scampering around

when a strange dog approached. He was a stocky fellow, bluey-grey in colour, with a wide head and a strong jaw. A thin white stripe ran down the centre of his face and his chest was white, as if he was wearing a bib. He was all muscle and must have weighed as much as Twiglet and Fennel put together.

His top lip curled in disgust.

'My territory,' he growled.

Sensing trouble, Twiglet moved quickly between Fennel and the new dog.

'It's OK. We were just leaving,' Twiglet explained, as calmly as he could.

But Fennel had no idea what was so dangerous. She knelt down on all fours and crawled towards the new dog.

'Park for sharing!' she said in Doggish.

The dog growled angrily.

'Are you disrespecting me?' he barked.

'Fennel, don't!' Rosie shouted anxiously. 'Just leave the nice dog alone and come back over here.

Both Fennel and Twiglet turned to look at Rosie, and at that moment, the big dog opened his huge jaws and launched himself at Fennel.

There was a terrifying blur of teeth as Twiglet threw himself into the path of the attack. In a split second he was on the ground, the muscular dog pinning him down.

The dog's owner sprinted over, looking shell-shocked as he tried to prize his animal's jaws apart.

'Tyson, release!' he said firmly, as if this had happened before.

After what seemed like an age, Tyson opened his jaws, leaving Twiglet limp and motionless on the ground. Rosie immediately picked him up and carried him to the car, Fennel following behind in speechless alarm.

'His collar saved him, no doubt about it,' said the vet. 'I've given him a couple of stitches on the back of his head and some painkillers, and here are some antibiotics he'll need for the next week, just to make sure the bite doesn't get infected. He's a very lucky boy.'

Rosie looked at the teeth marks on Twiglet's leather collar. If he hadn't been wearing it, the dog's teeth would have sunk into his neck. She couldn't bear to think about it.

'It's OK, Mummy,' Fennel said, stroking her arm. 'Twiglet's brave!'

'Yes, darling. Twiglet is brave. He's your guardian angel. Now, let's take him home and get him comfy.'

*

Fennel didn't leave Twiglet's side all night. She held his water bowl up to his face to make it easier for him to drink, and offered him soft, mushed-up food, putting it on the end of her finger so he didn't have to move.

'Please be all right, Twiggy,' she whispered in Doggish. 'Please be all right.'

Fennel slept beside Twiglet for seven nights. He was very weak for a few days and his wounds were sore, but eventually he recovered. The bond between him and Fennel was stronger than ever.

'I think Twiglet saved her life,' Rosie told Uncle James when he came to see the patient. 'I don't know what would have happened if he hadn't been there.'

'I'd heard about boxers being good guard dogs, but he is something else,' Uncle James replied. 'Twiglet really cares about Fennel. He'd do anything to protect her.'

Chapter Five

Starting School

Eventually, the time came for Fennel to start school. But on her first day she didn't seem excited at all. She dragged her heels and deliberately left her book bag behind to delay her departure.

Twiglet trotted down the stairs with her book bag in his mouth, dropping it at her feet with a shake of his head. He sat next to Fennel on the back seat of the car and tried to reassure her that everything would be OK.

'You've got to do this,' he woofed at her. 'You need to learn to read and write and add up numbers and do all the things that dogs can't do.'

'I don't want to,' Fennel whined quietly in Doggish. She glanced at her mum in the driver's seat, and leaned closer to Twiglet. 'I bet no one at school has any fun. They won't know how to wag their tails and they'll all smell funny.'

School turned out to be exactly as Fennel had feared. The other children didn't understand when she switched between English and Doggish, at break time no one would play fetch with her and the teachers told her she *had* to sit cross-legged like the rest of the class, not on her haunches. She missed Twiglet awfully.

'What's the matter, love?' Rosie said at home time as Fennel came out of school, her face red and blotchy. Fennel refused to talk about it. The next day, she started crying as soon as she got up and sniffled all the way to school.

Twiglet hated having to leave her there. He exchanged a forlorn look with Rosie as they watched her walk, shoulders slumped, through the school gates.

'I don't know what to do,' Rosie confided in Uncle James after a fortnight had passed with no improvement.

'Let me and Matt take her and Twiglet for a walk,' her brother suggested. 'If she's going to tell anyone what's the matter, she's likely to do it when she's out with Twiglet.'

So that weekend, Uncle James and Uncle Matt took Fennel and Twiglet for a gorgeous walk through the beech trees and down to the river. They played catch on the playing fields and Uncle James and Uncle Matt swung Fennel between them, flying her up into the air.

'How's school?' Uncle James asked lightly as they turned for home.

'Humph,' came the reply.

'I hated school to start with,' said Uncle Matt. 'There was a boy who told me I looked like a radish and made everyone else call me 'Radish'. One day, they left a whole pile of radishes in my book bag. I never really recovered from that; I still can't eat them!'

Fennel giggled. 'How could anyone think you looked like a radish?'

'It's just what some children do,' said Uncle James. 'It's all about power. If they see someone like you who's funny and bright and beautiful, they try to make you feel inferior. It's the worst side of human nature.'

'They say I'm weird because I sniffed them on my first day.' Fennel finally admitted. Twiglet walked close beside her to offer support and she reached out to stroke his head. 'Now whenever they see me, they bark and start chanting "Dog, dog, dog".'

'Well, I'd rather be a dog than a radish,' said Uncle Matt, so sincerely it made Fennel smile.

'I'd rather be a dog than a human being,' she replied.

Uncle James walked in silence for a few minutes.

'I've got an idea,' he said. 'Why don't we all try to be a dog for five minutes? Look at Twiglet – he's happy just being himself. He doesn't need to make another dog feel small to make himself look bigger.'

Twiglet wagged his tail happily. He was glad Uncle James had noticed his finest quality – that he was happy in his own skin.

'Let's do it now,' Uncle Matt suggested, running ahead of them. He zigged and zagged and looped back towards them, dive-bombing Fennel, who was in fits of laughter. She wagged her bottom and rolled on the grass before Uncle James sat on his haunches and tried to scratch his ear with his left foot.

'Cor, that's harder than it looks,' he chuckled as he fell over.

It was the first time Fennel had felt able to relax and have fun since school had started.

'You can do it every day,' Uncle James explained. 'Be a dog with Twiglet for five minutes in the morning and five minutes again in the evening. Then when you're at school you'll feel better about being a girl.'

'And if they call you "dog", just smile and say thank you,' advised Uncle Matt. 'It's their mistake to think it's an insult. You know it's really the biggest compliment of all, and if you take it that way, they'll soon get bored and move on to something else.'

Fennel nodded. 'I'll give it a try.'

'Good girl,' said Uncle James. 'Now, who's for hot chocolate?'

And her uncles took a hand each and swung Fennel home between them, with Twiglet trotting along behind.

Chapter Six

Fitness

It wasn't long before Fennel's school days became more bearable. She would have a few minutes of being extra dog-like with Twiglet each morning and, bit by bit, she found it easier to make new friends. In fact, her classmates soon started to appreciate Fennel's natural instinct for playing catch or piggy-in-the-middle, and applauded her when she made a particularly good save in football. But her friendship with Twiglet never wavered – and the two of them remained inseparable as the next few years went by.

One sunny day, just after Fennel had started Year Two, she had an idea. She and Twiglet were rolling around together in the park, while Grandma watched fondly from a bench. Fennel felt so proud of the connection she shared with Twiglet and how at ease they were around each other. She looked at her best friend, and announced quietly to him in Doggish: 'I want us to go to Crufts.'

Crufts was the biggest dog show in the world, and Fennel had been glued to the television for the whole of last year's competition at the Birmingham NEC.

Twiglet rolled on to his back and looked at her with curious eyes. She grinned and turned to her Grandma. 'Can we go to Crufts next year?' she said out loud.

'What a lovely idea!' Grandma exclaimed. 'What would you like to watch? The showing and the flyball?'

'I don't just want to watch,' Fennel said. 'I want us to compete!'

'Well, there's no harm in trying to enter,' said Grandma. 'I'll happily take you along. You'll have to qualify at the local show first, though, and you've only got six weeks to get in tip-top shape. You'd better start practising!'

And so, for the next few weeks, Fennel and Twiglet practised every day. Fennel trotted Twiglet up and down the sitting room. She put him on the kitchen table and examined him, feeling his teeth and under his tummy for any lumps or bumps. She groomed his coat until it gleamed.

When the day of the show came, Rosie gave

Fennel a long hug before she left to go to work. 'I'm so sorry I can't be there today, sweetheart.'

'That's all right, Mum,' Fennel replied. 'It's only the local show. You'll be there when we compete at Crufts!'

Twiglet gave a bark of agreement, and Rosie kissed them both on the tops of their heads.

'Of course I will. Good luck!'

When it comes to dog shows, there are very strict rules. Twiglet and Fennel were entered in the class for boxers, of course, and as the judge approached, Fennel did her best to make her face wrinkly and to adopt the broad-chested stance that judges look for in boxers.

There was a confusing moment as the judge went to examine Twiglet's teeth and found Fennel offering her mouth as well. He didn't

seem to know what to do, so he examined them both. The other owners tutted and shook their heads. Some of them laughed but Fennel didn't care.

They watched the rest of the competitors from the sidelines, excitement mounting. When it came to handing out the prizes, Fennel and Twiglet lined up expectantly.

Fennel knew she had shown herself and Twiglet as well as she possibly could and was very confident of receiving at least a commendation. The ringside announcer was calling forward people and their dogs to give them prizes. The list was getting longer and longer – and still their names had not been mentioned. Fennel started to worry. Maybe she had just made them both look stupid.

Finally, the last prize was handed out. They had won nothing. Fennel and Twiglet trudged back to Grandma, both their heads hung in disappointment.

'Oh, I'm sorry,' Fennel whispered. Twiglet nudged her hand with his nose.

'Don't worry, darlings,' said Grandma. 'At least you gave it a go.'

'But I so wanted us to go to Crufts together.' Fennel was speaking very softly and Grandma could barely hear her. 'I just wanted to show them what it's like to have a dog who is so understanding and kind.'

She smiled sadly at Twiglet, who licked her hand comfortingly.

As they walked back to the car, Fennel heard cheering. Twiglet heard it too and cocked his head. The noise was coming from an arena in the middle of the showground. They could hear an excited commentator and lots of people whooping and hollering.

'Do you want to go and have a look before we head home?' Grandma asked.

Fennel nodded – anything to take her mind off the embarrassment of the failed showing class. As they neared the arena, Fennel spotted lots of coloured poles arranged into mini show jumps. There was a red-and-black ramp going up steeply on one side and down the other, like a pointed bridge, a see-saw, a tunnel and a series of bendy poles.

'I think you'll enjoy this,' said Grandma.

They stood at the side of the arena for half an hour, watching dogs fly round the course, their owners pointing to jumps and encouraging them to go faster.

'It's amazing!' said Fennel excitedly. 'The dogs seem to know exactly where to go next and they're really enjoying it.'

'They love it,' said Grandma. 'It's very good for their fitness and you can see the good ones really work as a team with their owners.'

'A team,' repeated Fennel quietly. 'Yes, that's exactly what they are.'

The seed of an idea was planted and, by the time they got home, Fennel knew what she wanted to do.

'How did it go, darling?' asked her mum as they came inside.

'Oh, we didn't win anything,' replied

Fennel briskly. 'But it doesn't matter because I've got a better idea.'

Rosie looked at her daughter in astonishment.

'If you need me,' continued Fennel, 'I'll be in the garden. I need to build an agility course . . .'

Chapter Seven

Crufts

Fennel and Twiglet now had a new plan to get into Crufts: they would enter the agility competition. Fennel filled out all the paperwork and every day they practised in the garden. She dedicated her weekends and half-term holidays to training.

Fennel did all the jumping alongside

Twiglet, to make sure he knew exactly what he needed to do. She still moved very well on all fours, which was hardly surprising as she'd been doing it her whole life, so she started their first session by crawling through the tunnel to show Twiglet how it worked. At first, he'd followed slowly, but he soon got the hang of it and was able to jump and wriggle through the bendy poles too. He didn't much like heights, so the ramp was a problem, but Fennel raced up and down it herself to prove there was nothing to be afraid of. They got faster and fitter and more accurate every week, and by the time March came along they were flying through the course.

A week before Crufts, they got their official passes. Fennel felt a thrill as she looked at the bold green logo.

'We're nearly there, Twiggy!' she whispered

in Doggish as she stowed the pass in her pocket.

'So close!' he woofed back.

When the big day arrived, the whole family piled into the car and drove to the Birmingham NEC. Twiglet tried to distract Fennel from her nerves by doing accents. His German shepherd impression was excellent but his favourite impression was a dachshund. They have very deep voices but, because they're really small, the voice seems to come from the bottom of their tail. It's a tricky one to master but Twiglet was brilliant at it and Fennel giggled all the way.

After they'd found somewhere to park, the family started the long walk towards the NEC, with Fennel and Twiglet in the lead. There were dogs all around: some trotting beside their owners, others being carried and some on huge trolleys laden with brushes and blankets that were being wheeled towards the main entrance.

'It's the Utility and Toy Groups today,' Rosie read from her programme, as Twiglet paused to cock his leg against a tree. 'That's all the little dogs like chihuahuas, Pekingese, bichon frise and those gorgeous little fellows.'

She pointed to an Italian greyhound dancing past them on his toes. He looked so fragile that Twiglet feared his legs would break, but he seemed a bonny little thing.

'And what's in the Utility Group, Fennel?' Matt asked.

Fennel had been doing her homework so she knew the answer without looking at the programme.

'That's all the dogs that weren't bred for helping on a shoot or for herding animals, so it's got all sorts,' she said. 'Dalmatians, poodles, Tibetan terriers and schnauzers.'

'What group is Twiglet in?' Uncle James chimed in.

'Boxers are in the Working Group.'

'Really?' said Grandma. 'I always thought of them as wanting to play rather than work for a living.'

'They're really good guard dogs,' said Fennel, putting her arm around Twiglet. 'The best in the world, I'd say.'

'And from what I've seen, they're pretty good at agility,' her mum added proudly.

Fennel grinned. She couldn't believe how much improvement the two of them had made in such a short period of time. She was walking alongside Twiglet with such purpose that even Grandma noticed her confidence.

Fennel was perfectly at home, saying hello

to every dog they passed. Some of them looked a bit confused to hear a human speaking Doggish, but the poodles were particularly friendly. Fennel had always been told that they were intelligent dogs and now she believed it.

They had their passes checked as they went through the main entrance. While they waited for Rosie to fill out some forms, Fennel and Twiglet were distracted by the most magnificent pair of eyebrows. They sidled away from the rest of the family.

'Excuse me, but are you a schnauzer?' Fennel asked quietly in Doggish.

The grey-and-white dog in the queue behind them looked surprised but bowed his head politely.

'Indeed I am. Delighted to make your acquaintance. My name is Champion Count Basil of Bavaria.'

'Pleased to meet you, Count Basil! I'm Fennel and this is Twiglet,' said Fennel with a smile.

'And may I ask, what are you here for?'

'Agility,' Fennel answered.

The schnauzer raised his eyebrows to an even more pronounced height.

'Isn't that for the barking-mad collies?'

'Well, it is really, but there's a class called Medium ABC. We're in that,' Fennel explained.

'ABC? Is that some sort of spelling test?'

Twiglet smiled. He liked Count Basil.

'No, it stands for Anything But Collies,' Fennel clarified. 'What about you?'

'Oh, I'm here for the breed judging. If I win Best of Breed, I'll go through to the Group judging and then . . . who knows?'

Count Basil's owner darted over and tugged on his lead.

'There you are, Basil! Come on, time for action.'

Basil winked at Fennel and walked obediently behind his master. He swung his hips with the swagger of a catwalk model. Fennel gave him a big grin.

'Good luck to you both!' she heard him bark over his shoulder as they turned away.

Chapter Eight

Teamwork

There were five different halls at the NEC, all of them packed with people. They were either shopping for dog accessories, clothes or food, or watching the judging in the different arenas. Twiglet tried to stick close to Fennel as they squeezed through the crowds, heading towards the main arena. There they found their 'benches': low wooden shelves with dividers giving a bit of privacy from the dogs on either side. The noise was deafening. The collies were all shouting over each other and making no sense at all.

'What are they on about?' asked Fennel, her understanding of Doggish confused by the incessant yapping.

Twiglet listened carefully.

'It sounds like they're all just crying "Go, go, go!" over and over again,' Twiglet said.

When she saw them in action, Fennel understood why. These dogs had got themselves into a state of frenzy. Collies are made for agility in a way that neither Twiglet nor Fennel ever could be. They jigged and pranced like racehorses on the start line and, once the collies set off, their handlers only had to point towards a jump and they were over it, often racing on to the next obstacle before their owner had a chance to point the way.

'They're too fast for their own good,' said Fennel to her uncles, as they all watched one collie take the wrong course and get eliminated. 'We've got to be *accurate*. That's more important.'

Uncle James nodded at her proudly. 'That's the ticket!'

When it came to the ABC class, Twiglet checked out the opposition. There were a few cocker spaniels and a lot of mixed-breed dogs, who looked as if they were a bit of everything. Fennel walked the course, counting the strides between the jumps and noting the tricky switchback from the ramp to the jump before the bendy poles. She got down on all fours to measure the size of the tunnel in case it wasn't tall enough for Twiglet.

'Look at her,' said Uncle James. 'She knows

exactly what she needs to do.'

'She's so happy,' Grandma said, smiling. 'She was determined to get here in one class or another and I'm rather pleased it's agility instead of showing. Much more fun.'

Fennel looked up and grinned at her family.

Rosie gave her a quick wave. 'I'm so glad you're all here,' she said quietly to the others. 'This means the world to Fennel.'

'Oh, we're here to cheer, whatever happens!' said Uncle Matt. 'We'll be the loudest, most embarrassing fan club in Birmingham.'

It was nearly time to begin. Fennel was in the collecting area, waiting with the other competitors. She talked Twiglet through the course and they watched the first cocker spaniel set off. He was pretty good but he didn't put a foot on the white line at the end of the ramp, like he was supposed to, so he picked up a penalty.

'Next competitors: Twiglet and Fennel Wilson.'

The announcement caught them by surprise.

'But there's supposed to be someone else before us!' Fennel whispered to Twiglet anxiously.

'I guess they didn't turn up in time,' Twiglet murmured.

'Well, at least this means there's no time to get nervous . . .'

Fennel straightened her back and marched out with Twiglet trotting alongside her.

The announcer's voice boomed out of the speakers.

'Ladies and gentleman, please give a huge welcome to our youngest competitors: Fennel Wilson and her boxer, Twiglet!'

Fennel could hear Uncle James and Uncle Matt whistling and whooping from the stands. She looked up and smiled at them. The rest of the crowd politely clapped.

'This is what I wanted, more than anything,' Fennel said softly in Doggish as they crouched on the start line. 'To be here with you, Twiggy. Showing the world what a star you are.'

'We're a team,' Twiglet woofed, his face serious with concentration. 'Now let's show them what we can do!'

Fennel was nervous and excited, all in one bundle of butterflies.

'Ready?' she whispered.

Twiglet nodded. 'Let's go!'

The whistle went and they both reacted immediately.

Fennel sprinted into the centre of the course as she'd seen all the other owners do. Twiglet leaped over the first two jumps, darted up the ramp and down the other side, over another jump and through the bendy poles. He scooted through the tunnel and Fennel was there on the other side to point him to the next jump.

'I've never seen anything like it! They seem to be completely in tune!' shouted the commentator and the crowd started to roar.

But as Twiglet bounded over a pair of red-and-white poles, Fennel saw him throw her a worried look. The crowd was making such a racket she couldn't be sure, but she thought he was trying to say something to her in Doggish. She watched him bending and twisting through the course, eyes darting nervously up at her, and then she realized what the matter was. Whenever they'd done their training, they had run the obstacle course together. This was the first time Fennel hadn't been right there beside Twiglet – and it was making him anxious.

In an instant she knew what to do. *Don't*

worry, Twiglet! she thought. *We're a team!*

Fennel darted across the course to join Twiglet as he made a sharp right turn to a tyre jump. She threw herself through the hole in the middle of the tyre and beckoned him after her.

'Jump through!' shouted Fennel. 'Good boy!'

They took a turn back to the left and then two more jumps. The crowd was going wild and Fennel was sure she could hear Twiglet barking with excitement as they dashed round the course together.

'Well, this really is extraordinary,' cried the commentator. 'Twiglet the boxer is making record time and – can you believe it? – young Fennel is actually jumping the course too!'

The people in the collecting arena had stopped chatting and fussing over their own dogs, the crowds in the stands were cheering fit to burst and everyone was watching Twiglet and Fennel blazing their way round the course. Fennel even thought she caught a glimpse of Count Basil in the audience, barking his approval.

Fennel was beside Twiglet again and he woofed with delight as they leaped over the last two jumps side by side. Fennel threw herself over the line and Twiglet landed on top of her, licking her face. She couldn't believe that the deafening applause of the crowd was all for her and Twiglet. Rosie, Grandma, Uncle James and Uncle Matt were making more noise than anyone as the commentator said, 'Well that was a clear round for both Twiglet *and* Fennel in a very fast time of one minute and two seconds!'

Fennel and Twiglet ran over to where Rosie was waiting with her arms outstretched and a huge grin on her face.

'Well done!' she shrieked as she scooped Fennel off the floor. 'That was brilliant! You're the fastest so far.'

'Well done you too, old boy,' said Uncle James, giving Twiglet a rub.

'What a team you are!' cried Grandma. 'I'm *so* proud of you both.'

Uncle Matt patted Fennel on the head and said, 'I always said it was better to be a dog than a radish!'

Fennel and Twiglet settled down to watch the other competitors. The handlers were all much older than Fennel and positioned themselves in the middle of the course so they could direct their dogs. Fennel could see it was probably a more efficient method.

'But I reckon our way was more fun, don't you?' she laughed, and kissed Twiglet on the nose.

The whole family watched with their hearts in their mouths as the rest of the competitors made their runs. A cocker spaniel called Rufus was on course to beat their time until he stuttered at the last jump and knocked it down.

They were still in the lead . . . and there

was only one more dog to go!

That dog was a very fit looking Tibetan terrier called Pickle. He flew over the fences, but he hesitated at the top of the ramp. His owner managed to coax him down but he lost valuable time, even though he was much faster through the bendy poles and the tunnel than Fennel and Twiglet.

'This will be *very* close!' The commentator shouted. 'One minute and . . . *three* seconds,' he finished, as Pickle crossed the line.

Fennel's face was a picture. She and Twiglet had won! She was in such a state of shock that Twiglet had to jump up at her to bring her out of her daze. She took his front paws and they danced in a circle together, laughing. Fennel started to cry and Twiglet stopped to lick her cheek.

'Are you OK?' he asked.

Fennel leaned close to his ear. 'They're tears

of joy!' she whispered in Doggish. 'I wanted to compete at Crufts with you but I never thought we'd actually win!'

Chapter Nine

Champions

As they lined up to receive their prizes, Twiglet quietly asked Pickle the Tibetan terrier what had happened at the top of the ramp.

'My owner thinks it's nerves, but the truth is, I don't like heights,' he explained. 'It doesn't matter, though; I'm glad you won. Your owner seems to really understand you.'

'Thank you,' said Fennel in Doggish.

'What's that, dear?'

Fennel looked up to see Pickle's owner, a pretty lady about her mum's age, looking curiously down at her.

'It's just . . .' she held the woman's gaze. 'Pickle's frightened of heights. That's why he froze on the top of the ramp.'

The woman raised her eyebrows. 'Do you really think so? Now that you mention it, I do remember a bad experience a few years ago when he got stuck in a treehouse. Perhaps that would explain it.'

Fennel nodded. 'That makes sense.'

The woman laid a gentle hand on her arm.

'I'm ever so impressed with your teamwork. You really do understand your dog!'

Fennel grinned and Twiglet gave a happy bark.

'I wouldn't be at all surprised if you grew

up to be a dog whisperer,' the woman chuckled.

Fennel looked at her in surprise. 'A dog whisperer?'

'Yes! That's the name for someone who really understands dogs and can communicate with them like nobody else. It's a very special thing.'

Fennel felt her heart swell with pride but before she could respond, the announcer called her name, and it was time for her and Twiglet to collect their first prize.

'Come on,' said Fennel out loud, leading Twiglet forward. 'We deserve this!'

'Who was that lady you were talking to earlier?' Rosie asked, after the prize ceremony had finished.

'That was Pickle's owner,' replied Fennel. 'I told her that Pickle is frightened of heights.

Of course, I didn't tell her that I can speak Doggish!'

Her family stared at her in surprise. 'What do you mean, you can speak Doggish?' said Uncle James.

'Oh!' Fennel reddened. She'd said more than she'd meant to. 'I just mean that I can sometimes understand what dogs are saying. Not all the time, just the obvious things.'

Her mother and grandmother exchanged a look.

'Is that so?' said Rosie. 'I did wonder. There was that time a few weeks after Twiglet had been bitten by that big dog – we all thought he had recovered but you told me that his neck still hurt.'

'Yes,' agreed Grandma. 'And I heard you making strange noises to Twiglet when you were training in the garden. I wondered what you were up to!'

'You'll have to be careful, you know,' said Rosie. 'It's a gift that not everyone will understand.'

'I know that,' said Fennel. 'And I know that you've all been worried that I think I'm a dog. I know I'm not. Much more importantly – I know what I am! I'm a dog *whisperer.*'

'That sounds like a job that was made for you,' Rosie said with a smile.

They were passing the prize-giving for Best of Breed, and Twiglet gave a bark as he spotted their friend Basil through the crowd. Basil's owner was stepping up to take first prize!

'Oh, Mum, please can we watch?' Fennel pleaded.

'Of course, darling,' Rosie replied, ruffling her hair. 'Anything for my champions!'

They watched with delight as Basil

advanced into the Group judging and cheered loudly when he won that too. Next up was Best in Show, the grand final of Crufts. Twenty-two thousand dogs had been judged and now it was down to the final seven. Fennel and Twiglet stood close together as they watched, breathless with anticipation.

The judge went slowly down the line of dogs, the crowd following his every move. Eventually he stopped, stepped back . . . and pointed at Basil.

The crowd went wild. Fennel clapped and whistled, and Twiglet barked beside her. Count Basil was the Champion of Crufts – the best of the best!

As Basil and his owner were encircled by a scrum of excited friends and family, Fennel and Twiglet heard him give a loud, joyful howl.

'That's for my new friends!' he barked out in Doggish. 'For Twiglet and Fennel, the best team I've ever seen!'

THE END

If you enjoyed reading about Fennel's special relationship with Twiglet, you'll love the story of suffragette Emmeline Pankhurst and her adventures with a little puppy called Rascal. Turn the page for a sneak preview . . .

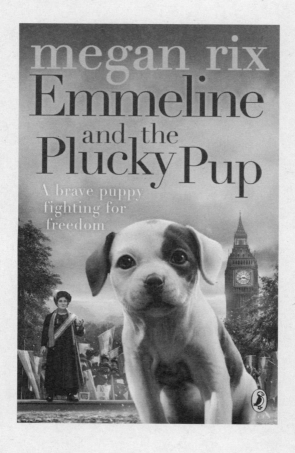

megan rix

Emmeline and the Plucky Pup

A brave puppy fighting for freedom

Chapter 1
November 1910

The little Staffordshire bull terrier puppy's shiny black nose sniffed at the delicious smells drifting on the cold November air. The puppy was very thin and its ribs were easy to see through its white, brown and black fur.

'Jellied eels – get your jellied eels here!'

'Baked potatoes! Hot baked potatoes!'

'Oysters and whelks! Best oysters and whelks!'

'Chestnuts! Hot chestnuts!'

It was after one o'clock and lots of hungry people were buying food from the stalls and handcarts in Parliament Square Garden, across the road from the Houses of Parliament. No one was taking much notice of the thin little puppy as it trotted round the stalls.

'Meat pies!' called a vendor.

'I'll have two pies,' a man said.

As the man bit into the first pie the puppy looked up at him and gave a whine.

'Get out of it, you,' the man said, some gravy from the pie running down his chin.

A handbell clanged behind them. 'Muffins! Freshly baked muffins!'

The puppy looked longingly at the tray of muffins balanced on the baker's head. But none of the muffins fell off and the baker went on his way ringing his bell.

'Sheep's trotters – fresh sheep's trotters!' a

red-faced stallholder shouted to passers-by.

The puppy drooled at the delicious meaty smell.

'Are they really fresh?' a woman asked.

'Won't find fresher,' the stallholder replied.

Seizing its moment, the desperate puppy stood on its hind legs and bit into a cooked sheep's trotter from the edge of the stall.

'Hey, you! Come back here!' the stallholder shouted as the tiny dog tore off with it. 'Thief, thief!'

'I'll catch him,' yelled one of the errand boys who was hanging around the stalls hoping for work.

'Penny if you do,' said the stallholder. 'But be quick.'

'I'll be quicker than him,' said a second boy.

'Penny for whoever brings it back,' the stallholder told them.

A third, fourth, fifth and sixth boy joined in the chase. Everyone wanted the penny. They sped across the grass after the puppy, who had the warm sheep's trotter clamped in its jaws.

The puppy darted in and out of the legs of people. The boys followed, weaving in and out and trying not to trip or bump into anyone. The square was full of tourists marvelling at the majestic Houses of Parliament, where the laws of the land were made.

'Hello, puppy, that looks tasty!' Police Constable Tom Smith laughed as the small piebald dog ran between his legs. He and an elderly constable called Purvis were on their way to join the police officers lining the roads around Parliament Square Garden.

'Don't worry about that now,' Constable Purvis said, as the puppy ran into a bush to devour its prize. 'You don't want to be late, not today. We've got important work to do.'

Tom nodded and they walked on. He'd barely been able to sleep last night, he'd been so excited. It was his first day on duty as a police constable and he was going to be protecting the Houses of Parliament, because there was going to be a suffragette march. The suffragettes were campaigning for women to have the right to vote, just like men, and Tom knew that they were willing to use force. A couple of years ago there'd been a mass rally in Hyde Park with over 300,000 suffrage supporters. That one had been peaceful because it had been led by the suffragists rather than the suffragettes. Suffragists wanted the same thing as the suffragettes but they went about trying to get it by peaceful campaigning. Suffragettes were more militant. They'd attacked a member of Parliament – Mr Churchill – and rang a muffin bell continually when he'd tried to make a speech. They'd smashed the windows of 10 Downing Street, where the prime minister lived, and two of them had even chained themselves to the railings outside, in protest at the government not giving them the vote.

Tom didn't know how many women would be marching today. But the papers were full of the news that the prime minister, Mr Asquith, had gone back on his word that women who owned property and were over thirty years old would be given the vote, so there might be lots of protestors. The police had to be ready. Tom was feeling a little nervous, even though he was one of many officers: the Home Secretary, Mr Winston Churchill, had asked for six thousand policemen from all over the country to come to London and protect the Palace of Westminster. Most of them were on foot, but some looked very fierce mounted on huge police horses.

They all stood to attention as the police commissioner gave them his orders: 'The job of the police is to keep everyone calm. Crowds need to be controlled or members of the public could easily be hurt if the protest gets out of control.'

'There, it's in that bush!' Tom heard an errand boy shout as he and Constable Purvis moved to their positions across the road. He watched as the group of boys charged towards the little puppy, who ran out of the bush, across the grass and away.

WORLD
BOOK
DAY

Hello

We hope you enjoyed this book.

Proudly brought to you by **WORLD BOOK DAY**,

the **BIGGEST CELEBRATION** of the **magic** and **fun** of **storytelling**.

We are the **bringer of books to readers** everywhere

and a **charity** on a **MISSION**

to take you on a **READING JOURNEY**.

EXPLORE
new worlds
(and bookshops!)

EXPAND
your
imagination

DISCOVER
some of the very
best authors and
illustrators with us.

A **LOVE OF READING** is one of life's greatest gifts.

And this book is **OUR gift to YOU**.

HAPPY READING.
HAPPY WORLD BOOK DAY!

WORLD BOOK DAY

SHARE A STORY

Discover and share stories from breakfast to bedtime.

THREE ways to continue YOUR reading adventure

1 VISIT YOUR LOCAL BOOKSHOP

Your go-to destination for awesome reading recommendations and events with your favourite authors and illustrators.

FIND YOUR LOCAL BOOKSHOP

booksellers.org.uk/ bookshopsearch

2 JOIN YOUR LOCAL LIBRARY

Browse and borrow from a huge selection of books, get expert ideas of what to read next and take part in wonderful family reading activities – all for FREE!

FIND YOUR LOCAL LIBRARY

findmylibrary.co.uk

3 GO ONLINE AT WORLDBOOKDAY.COM

Fun podcasts, activities, games, videos, downloads, competitions, new books galore and all the latest book news.

SPONSORED BY

NATIONAL BOOK tokens

Illustrations © Jim Field

Celebrate stories. Love reading.